Francine, Believe It or Not

A Marc Brown ARTHUR Chapter Book

Francine, Believe It or Not

Text by Stephen Krensky
Based on a teleplay by Joe Fallon

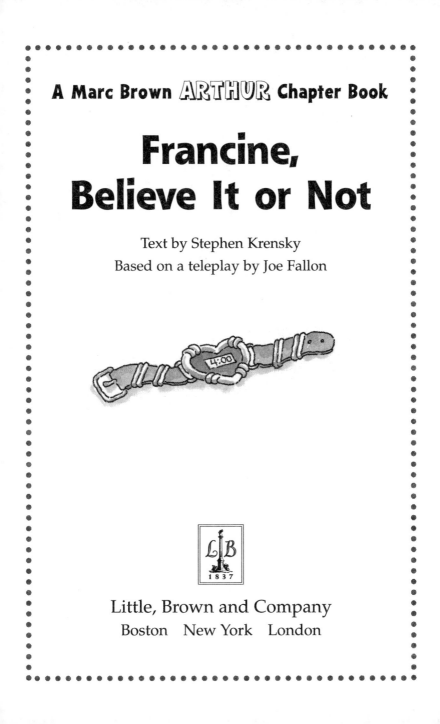

Little, Brown and Company
Boston   New York   London

For my sister Bonnie,
the inspiration for Francine

Chapter 1

. . . .

"Over here, Francine!"

Arthur was calling for a pass in the middle of a street hockey game. He and Francine were on a team with Muffy, Buster, Sue Ellen, and the Brain. The other team, led by Binky, included Molly, Kiefer, Mona, Speedy, and Rattles.

Francine didn't seem to hear Arthur's call. She faked Molly to the left, took two long strides, and fired at the goal.

Rattles was the opposing goalie. He tried to block the puck—and missed.

"Score!" cried Francine.

Binky controlled the face-off and brought the puck back into play. He skated past Buster, but Francine poke-checked the puck between his legs.

Buster raced down the sideline. "I'm free, Francine, I'm free!" he shouted.

But Francine paid no attention. Instead of making the long open pass to Buster, she swept around Kiefer and came in hard on Rattles, firing another shot.

This one bounced off the post.

The puck ricocheted back to Arthur. He steadied it, getting ready to move.

Then Francine stole it away. She moved in quickly—and scored!

"Hey!" Arthur shouted. "I'm on your team!"

"You were taking too long," she told him. "Do you want to win or not? I mean, look—we're doing great. Now the score's tied, three to three."

"Who's we?" said Muffy. "Nobody but you gets to do anything."

Francine shrugged. As far as she was concerned, there was nothing wrong with that.

During a time-out, the team huddled to discuss strategy.

"Don't you think we could show a little more teamwork?" asked the Brain.

"I agree," said Francine.

"You do?" said Arthur.

"Absolutely. You guys are not getting me the puck fast enough."

"I don't think that's what the Brain meant," said Arthur.

"Hey, Binky's team is tough," Francine reminded them. "I'll gladly give you the puck if everybody wants to lose."

Arthur and the others looked shocked.

"Francine Frensky!" said Muffy. "I

think you're the rudest person I've ever met."

Francine shrugged. "I guess the truth hurts."

Muffy looked ready to explode.

Everyone got back into position for the face-off. A little later, Muffy got a pass right near the goal.

"Shoot, shoot!" cried Arthur.

"No!" said Francine. "Pass it to me!"

Muffy hesitated. She looked down at the puck and then up at Francine. Shaking her head, she swung back her stick to shoot.

And Molly stole the puck. She pivoted around and took three long strides toward the opposite goal. Then she slapped a shot into the net just as the whistle blew.

"Score!" said Binky. "We win, four to three!"

Francine threw her stick down on the

ground. "I can't believe it. We were *sooooo* close." She turned to Arthur. "I hope you're happy, Mr. Fairness."

"Me?" said Arthur. "What did I do?"

Francine snorted. "You told Muffy to shoot. You know what a bad shot she is."

Muffy turned away sharply so no one could see her face. Then she slowly skated away.

"We're just lucky there's another play-off game next week," said Francine. She looked around. "Where'd Muffy go?"

"I think she'd heard enough," said Arthur.

"So have we," said Buster.

The rest of the team walked away, leaving Francine standing alone.

Chapter 2

When Francine took a moment to think about it, she decided that something was bothering her friends. Muffy had seemed more than a little upset, and everyone else had been a bit grumpy, too.

I know it bothers them that we lost, she thought. But they have to stay tough. They need to be more like me.

Still, Muffy was her best friend, and Francine didn't want her to suffer in silence. So she got on her bike and raced after Muffy.

"Wait up!" Francine called out.

Muffy was walking along at a fast clip,

and she didn't slow down at the sound of Francine's voice.

"Didn't you hear me?" asked Francine, coming up beside her.

Muffy kept on walking. "Yes, I heard you," she said.

"But you didn't stop."

"Why should I?" asked Muffy, without slowing down a bit. "I can imagine what you're going to say. I'm sure there's something wrong with the way I walk. Too big a stride? Or too little? Or maybe my walking is too hopeless for improvement? Perhaps you think it would be better if I stopped walking altogether and let *you* do my walking for me."

Francine braked to a stop. "You can't fool me, Muffy. You're mad about something."

Muffy stopped, too. She stared hard at Francine. "Mad? Why should I be mad?

Oh, yes, now I remember. You said I cost us the game."

"Well, didn't you?"

Muffy walked up to Francine, nose to nose. "Whether I did or I didn't, that's no way to talk. We're supposed to be a team, remember? Honestly, Francine, sometimes you're like a nonstop insult machine."

"What?" Francine was shocked. "How can you say that? I'm one of the nicest people in the whole school."

"You think so?" Muffy snapped. "Then prove it. I'll bet you this Princess Peach watch that you're wrong."

Muffy held out her arm. "This is the deluxe model, of course—with the combination stopwatch and odometer."

Francine sighed. "You know I've wanted one of those watches from the first moment I saw them advertised on TV."

"True," said Muffy. "And since they're

so expensive, this is your best chance to own one."

"What's the bet, then?" Francine asked.

Muffy folded her arms. "It's simple. I'll bet you can't be nice for one entire week."

"Me? Nice?" Francine started to laugh. "That's a sucker bet. I could do that in my sleep."

"I'm sure you could," said Muffy. "But this is harder—because you have to do it while you're awake. Oh, and one other thing . . ."

"Aha!" said Francine. "Here comes the small print."

"Not really," said Muffy. "It's just that you can't tell anyone. If you did, they might try to help you."

Francine waved her arm. "That's no big deal. I'm so nice anyway, they won't even notice the difference."

"We'll see," said Muffy. "We'll see."

Chapter 3

. . . .

The next morning, the kids arrived at school in a rush, filling the halls like ants scurrying into an anthill.

Usually, Arthur hated the feeling of being crushed in a crowd, but today he welcomed the camouflage. He tried to move as fast as possible.

As the kids began to separate, Arthur reached his locker.

"Whoa!" said Buster, stepping in front of him. "Alert the fashion police!" He circled Arthur slowly. "Okay, fess up. Where did you get that weird sweater?"

Arthur looked down and sighed. He

had been hoping to stash the sweater in his locker before anyone got a look. But he hadn't been that lucky. The sweater was one-of-a-kind. It was covered with bright slashes of orange, green, and purple, which crisscrossed the front and back like tire tracks.

Buster took a closer look. "I've seen car accidents that looked better than this," he said.

Arthur shuddered. "My aunt Bonnie got it for me. It was handmade, she said. Over many months. By workers —"

"Who kept their eyes shut?" said Buster.

"Maybe," said Arthur. "But my other one is dirty, so my mom dragged this out of the closet."

Buster looked over Arthur's shoulder. "Uh-oh! You'd better get it off fast. Here comes Francine. If she sees this eyesore, you'll never hear the end of it."

But it was already too late. Francine's face had broken into a wide grin.

"Arthur, that sweater, it's—"

She looked up to see Muffy hold out her arm and glance at her watch.

"You were saying, Francine?" Muffy asked.

"Um, it's nice, Arthur. Very nice. And colorful."

Arthur and Buster looked stunned. "Are you feeling all right, Francine?" asked Buster.

Of course," said Francine. Then she quickly walked away.

Later at recess, the kids were playing baseball. The game was a close one, and Francine's team was up. Arthur and the Brain were already at first and third. Francine was on deck, and it was Buster's turn at the plate.

"Ah, Buster," said Francine, "can I bat for you?"

"Why?" asked Buster.

"Well," said Francine, "this is a crucial situation. We have a chance to take the lead, so . . ." Her voice trailed off as she noticed Muffy inspecting her watch again.

"So . . . *what?*" asked Buster.

"Um, so I just want to make sure you're up for the challenge. It's a big moment. You look a little tired. Do you feel okay?"

"Yeah, I'm fine," said Buster. "In the pink. Fit as a fiddle. Now, if you'll excuse me . . ."

He headed for the plate.

"Good. Glad to hear it," Francine called after him. "Now, go get 'em!"

Arthur and the Brain exchanged surprised looks. "I never expected to see Francine turn down the chance to speak her mind," said the Brain.

"And that's *twice* in one day," added Arthur.

They looked at each other and scratched their heads.

Clearly, the world was full of surprises.

Chapter 4

• • • • • • • • • • • •

If either Arthur or the Brain thought that the mystery surrounding Francine's behavior would clear up quickly, they were wrong. In fact, the mystery only grew with each passing day.

The next instance occurred over the weekend. Arthur, Buster, and Sue Ellen were playing in the park when the Brain came running up to them. "Follow me!" he said, huffing and puffing. "You have to see this."

They went back to the school playground.

"Take a look around the corner of the

building," said the Brain. "Just your heads, though—to make sure you're not seen."

Arthur, Buster, and Sue Ellen did what he said.

"I can't believe it," said Arthur.

"Amazing," added Buster.

"Something to tell my grandchildren," Sue Ellen declared.

They watched silently as Francine and Muffy practiced street hockey. That in itself was not unusual, but the action and conversation were far from normal.

Francine was demonstrating how to change direction with the puck. She glided up and down, keeping her stick in front of her and knocking the puck back and forth.

"Okay," she told Muffy, "now you try it."

Muffy tried her best, but she couldn't hold the turn. The puck went skidding

away, and she collided with Francine, knocking her down.

"Muffy, can't you do anything" — Francine stopped herself—"wrong? That was almost perfect."

"I'm glad you're taking this so well," said Muffy. "But I need to tell you . . ." She pointed at Francine's leg.

Francine looked down. There was a new hole in her pants at the knee.

"My good pants!" she gasped.

"Sorry," said Muffy. "It was an accident. Am I still invited over for dinner?"

Francine swallowed deeply. "Yes," she said. "Friends don't let ripped pants come between them."

Muffy started to leave, and Francine began kicking the brick wall. Being nice was harder than she had expected.

She stopped abruptly when Muffy turned around, saw Francine, and pointed to her watch. "I'll see you at five-thirty," she said.

"I'll be waiting," said Francine.

"You know," Muffy added, "there are four days, nine hours, and twenty-seven minutes left. Want to call the bet off?"

Francine shook her head. "Don't worry about me. Just take good care of my watch."

Arthur and the other kids turned away. They couldn't hear everything Francine and Muffy had said, but they had heard enough.

"*Weird*," said Buster.

"Extremely weird," the Brain added.

"Francine just hasn't been herself lately," said Arthur. "Has anybody else noticed?"

Everyone nodded.

"Definitely," said the Brain. "She actually

replaced my football—the one she threw down the sewer last week."

"Well, listen to this," said Sue Ellen. "She came to my house early yesterday morning with a carton of orange juice. She said it was to replace a glass she drank last summer without asking."

"I said it before," said Buster, "and I'll say it again. *Weird. Weird. Weird. Weird.*"

Nobody could argue with him.

Chapter 5

· · · · · · · · · · · ·

"This is delicious," said Francine, eating another spoonful.

The Frenskys were having dinner. Mr. and Mrs. Frensky sat at opposite ends of the table. Francine and her sister, Catherine, sat between them. Muffy was there, too, sitting next to Francine as her guest.

"What is it *exactly* you find delicious?" Catherine asked.

"Oh," said Francine, "the creamed corn, the stew . . ."

"I thought you hated creamed corn," said Catherine.

Francine tried to smile. "Really? I don't remember that."

"People change," Muffy said brightly. "Happens all the time."

Catherine looked around. "Not in this family."

"This certainly is fancy," said Mr. Frensky, trying to change the subject. He was staring at his paper napkin, which Muffy had folded into the shape of a swan.

"Oliver," said Mrs. Frensky, "your napkin belongs on your lap."

"I know, I know," said her husband. "But Muffy did such a great job folding them, I wanted to admire mine. I can't do that if it's hiding under the table."

"Well, there's some stew on your chin," said Mrs. Frensky. "Why don't you use your swan to clean it up."

When the meal ended, Mr. Frensky started to clear the dishes from the table.

Muffy cleared her throat and raised an eyebrow at Francine.

"Father," Francine said suddenly, "let me get those for you."

Mr. Frensky froze in shock. "What? Who said that?"

"I did," said Francine.

Mr. Frensky frowned. "You look like my daughter Francine," he said. "And your voice is similar. But . . ."

"Are you trying to discourage me?" Francine asked.

Her father rubbed his chin. "I see your point. Well, carry on. And keep up the good work!"

Francine smiled — and filled her arms with dishes. Then she carried them into the kitchen.

Catherine followed her.

"So what's the deal here?" she asked.

"Deal?" said Francine. "What deal?"

"This sudden change. This transformation."

Francine shrugged. "I don't know what you mean," she said, beginning to load the dishwasher.

"You're being so helpful, so complimentary. It's out of character."

Francine snorted. "You don't know me as well as you think. I'm just trying to be a good host."

Catherine laughed. "Really? Well, before you start changing your manners, you might consider working on your wardrobe. I mean, you're wearing ripped pants."

"So what?" said Francine. "For your information, *your* clothes—"

Just then, Muffy came in, folding another swan. "Your father asked me to make him a whole little family," she explained. Then she looked at Francine. "Sorry. I didn't mean to interrupt."

Francine took a deep breath. "What I was saying, Catherine, was that your clothes . . . are great. In fact, I wish I had more like them myself. Maybe you could take me shopping sometime."

Catherine looked shocked. "Finally," she declared, "you display some taste and good sense. I wouldn't have thought it possible. Maybe there's hope for you yet. We'll go next weekend."

Francine smiled until Catherine walked out. Then she clenched her fists. Francine was tough, but even she wasn't sure how much more of this she could take.

Chapter 6

• • • • • • • • • • •

In the school cafeteria, Arthur, the Brain, Buster, and Sue Ellen were huddled around a table.

"Then we agree," said Arthur.

The others nodded.

"Francine's become friendly, helpful, and pleasant," Arthur went on. "It doesn't feel right. It's creepy."

"The situation may be even worse than that," said the Brain. "I would guess that this change has thrown the equilibrium in the universe completely out of whack. It could have very serious consequences."

"Like what?" asked Buster.

The Brain thought about it for a moment. "A change like this represents a dramatic shift in energy. On the other side of the galaxy, there could be stars winking out just to keep things even."

"Wow!" said Buster. "So if this kept up, the whole nighttime sky could go dark."

"Calm down, Buster," said Sue Ellen. "We may not be dealing with a problem like that. After all, we don't know for sure that this is the real Francine."

"We don't?" said Arthur.

Sue Ellen shook her head. "You said yourself she seems entirely different. What if she *is?*" Sue Ellen lowered her voice. "Maybe she's been replaced by an alien who's disguising itself in Francine's body." She paused. "Or I suppose she could be a look-alike robot that hasn't been properly programmed."

"Whatever she is, she *scares* me!" said Buster.

"We're all scared," said Arthur.

"And worried," said the Brain. "Even if the universe is not at risk, such behavior is no good for Francine. It's not natural. Allow me to demonstrate."

He picked up an unopened soda bottle.

"Imagine that this bottle is Francine," he said.

"Really?" said Buster. "I think her head is bigger."

"True," the Brain admitted, "but try and get past that. Now, Francine is the bottle, and the soda is her personality bottled up inside it. If someone with her temper is holding it in, the pressure will build."

He shook the bottle.

"And the longer she holds her anger in, the more the pressure will build up."

He shook the bottle harder.

"Until she reaches the point where the pressure will be too much to contain any longer."

He untwisted the bottle cap, and the soda shot out.

Everyone gasped.

Arthur watched the soda fizzle around the bottle. He imagined Francine foaming at the mouth.

"We can't let this happen," he said.

"It would be very messy," said Buster. "We've got to help Francine before she pops."

"But how?" asked Sue Ellen.

"I have a plan," said the Brain. "We have to find a way to make her lose her temper. I admit there's a chance of personal risk. So if anyone wants to back out, now's the time."

Nobody moved.

"Then we'll do it," said the Brain. "And

remember, it's for her own good. Once the pressure is released, the danger will pass."

"For her, anyway," said Buster. "But I may never drink another bottle of soda again."

Chapter 7

• • • • • • • • • • •

Arthur and Buster got the chance to put the Brain's plan into operation the next day. They were playing in the outfield during a baseball game. Francine was pitching as usual.

Sue Ellen was up at bat. She hit Francine's first pitch toward right center field. It was a deep pop fly, and both Arthur and Buster had plenty of time to get under it.

"This is an easy one," Arthur told Buster. "If we miss it, Francine's bound to go crazy."

The boys came together but stopped short as the ball fell in front of them.

Francine put her face in her glove.

"Get ready," said Arthur. "She's ready to explode."

"I wish I had earplugs," said Buster. "I just know she's going to scream."

Francine took a deep breath and looked up.

"I guess the sun was in your eyes," she called out to them. "We'll get the next one."

"Now what?" said Buster.

"We go to Phase Two," said Arthur.

"What's that?" Buster asked.

"I'll let you know when I think of it."

After the game, everyone went to the Sugar Bowl for a snack. Buster, Arthur, and the Brain were already seated when Sue Ellen, Muffy, and Francine came in.

"You got here fast," said Francine.

"We were thirsty," said Buster.

"But we didn't forget our friends," said Arthur. "Here, Francine, we bought you a soda."

"Thanks, Arthur. I think I could drink a tub of anything right now."

She started to take a long drink.

"Phase Two," Arthur whispered to Buster.

Suddenly, Francine pulled back from the glass.

"A-Arthur!" she sputtered. "This is cherry! You *know* I don't like cherry!"

Arthur just waved his hand. "What's the big deal? Isn't it time you broadened your horizons?"

He prepared himself for the volcano to erupt.

But Francine only sighed. "Maybe you're right. I should give it another chance."

She took another sip, gritting her teeth all the while.

Buster looked shocked, but he still spoke up.

"Um, Francine," he said, "I heard Binky say he could beat you at any sport, any day."

"He did?" Francine raised an eyebrow.

"Doesn't that make you mad?" said Arthur.

"Mad enough to go find him?" said the Brain. "And maybe beat him at some game to teach him a lesson?"

Francine shook her head. "Oh, no. Don't be silly. Maybe he's bragging because he's insecure. Or maybe he's been practicing really hard and *can* beat me. Come on, girls, let's find a table to ourselves. These guys are clearly in a mean mood."

She led the other girls away.

The three boys shook their heads.

"Well, we tried," said the Brain.

"I hate to think of all the pressure building up," said Arthur.

"She could burst at any time," said Buster.

He saw himself in class, watching Francine. Suddenly, her face turned very red—and then her head popped off her shoulders. It rocketed up through the ceiling and up into the sky.

"Well, if she does," said Arthur, "I hope we're there to pick up the pieces."

Chapter 8

● ● ● ● ● ● ● ● ● ● ●

Arthur and Buster were standing outside Muffy's house. Francine had kept up her strange behavior for six days straight. Everyone figured she couldn't go on much longer.

"I still don't see why we're here," said Buster. "We could be trying other ways of making Francine mad. We could put itching powder in her socks or repeat everything she says or—"

Arthur shook his head. "We've tried that kind of stuff already. It's not working. There may be something else going on here."

He rang the bell.

"But why ask Muffy?" said Buster. He rubbed his neck and looked around at the shiny limousine in the driveway and the fancy flowers bordering the lawn. "Besides, whenever I come to her house, I always feel like I should be wearing fancy, scratchy clothes."

"Never mind that," said Arthur. "Muffy is Francine's best friend. She may be able to help."

Muffy answered the door.

"Hi, Muffy," said Arthur. Then he paused. Although it had been his idea to consult Muffy, he wasn't sure what he should say exactly. "Nice day, isn't it?"

Muffy looked up at the sky. Then she smiled at Arthur. "I guess so. Did you come all the way over here just to give me a weather report?"

"Um, not exactly."

"I like your new sneakers," Buster put

in. He didn't look any more comfortable than Arthur.

Muffy nodded. "Thanks. I got them yesterday. But I didn't think you paid attention to those things, Buster."

"Not always," Buster admitted. "But it's good to stay in training in case I have to solve any more mysteries."

"Speaking of mysteries," said Arthur, "that's really why we came. Have you noticed the way Francine has been acting lately?"

Muffy blinked. "What do you mean?"

"You must have noticed," said Arthur. "After all, you are her best friend. She's been so polite and helpful — hardly like the real Francine at all."

"I may have noticed *something* . . . ," said Muffy. "But I don't think it's anything to worry about."

"We do," said Buster. He told her about the Brain's soda bottle theory.

Muffy looked at her watch.

"Don't worry," she said. "She'll be back to normal by this time tomorrow afternoon."

Arthur looked surprised. "How do you know *that?*" he asked.

"I just do. That's all I can say."

Arthur nodded. He didn't care what kind of secret the girls were keeping as long as Francine would get back to normal soon. "You mean right after the street hockey game?"

Muffy looked surprised. "The game! I'd forgotten about the game!"

"Are you all right, Muffy?" asked Arthur. "All of a sudden you look sort of pale."

"Like a vampire victim," Buster added.

"I'm fine," said Muffy. "Really. I just hope we don't lose tomorrow."

Arthur and Buster looked at each other. "Yeah, me, too," they both said together.

Chapter 9

• • • • • • • • • • •

The game the next day was not going well, at least not for Arthur's team. Late in the action, Binky got a pass right in front of the goal. Francine was in front of him. Binky expected her to try to knock the puck away or at least distract him by making faces.

But Francine just stood there.

Binky wound up to shoot — and Francine didn't even try to stop him.

Score!

"All right!" Binky shouted. "That puts us ahead."

"Francine!" Arthur whispered. "What

are you doing? Why didn't you try to stop Binky?"

"I didn't want to be rude," said Francine. "It would hurt his feelings."

"Aargh!" Muffy cried—and buried her face in her hands.

As play continued, Francine was always near the action but never in the middle of it. At one point, Binky raced toward her with the puck—and Francine moved out of his way.

"Excuse me," she said.

On the next play, Muffy had the puck in scoring position.

"Help her, Francine!" cried Arthur. "Give her someone to pass to."

"Muffy's entitled to a chance to shoot," said Francine.

"But she's a terrible shot," Arthur whispered.

"She'll never get any better if she

doesn't get the chance to practice." Francine waved to Muffy. "Go ahead!"

Muffy nodded. She pulled her stick back and fired the puck.

Score!

"Good shot, Muffy!" said Francine. "Way to go!"

But Francine was just as helpful to the other team. A few minutes later, she had the puck near her own team's goal. Kiefer came up to guard her.

Francine smiled at him. "Kiefer, you haven't scored a goal all season, have you?"

"Ummm . . . no."

"Don't you think it would feel pretty good?"

Kiefer hesitated. "Is this some kind of trick?"

Francine passed him the puck. "Not at all. Go ahead, take a shot."

Kiefer didn't wait to hear any more. The puck was on his stick, and he had a clear shot.

Score!

"Francine!" yelled Buster. "What are you doing?"

"Just trying to be encouraging," she called out.

During a time-out, Francine sipped some water. Muffy sat down beside her.

"Francine, there's only thirty-seven minutes left in the bet. The game will be over before then. I want to declare you the winner now."

"Now, Muffy, you know that's not right," said Francine. "I can last thirty-seven more minutes. Besides, you were right. Everyone plays better if I'm nice."

Muffy grabbed her by the shirt and pulled her closer.

"Everyone *including* the other team."

She took off her watch and held it out.

"Here. Take the watch. Now, snap out of it and get mean."

"Thank you for the watch," Francine said politely, "but I still feel I should last the *whole* seven days. After all, a bet's a bet."

"I can't believe this!" said Muffy.

"You might as well give up now," Binky called out. "We're so far ahead, you can never catch up."

As he skated past them, he accidentally bumped into Francine. The collision knocked the watch out of Francine's hand.

It fell to the ground—and Binky fell on top of it.

Crunnncchhhh!

"My watch!" cried Francine.

"What about me?" asked Binky. "I think I heard some bones break."

"Never mind about you and your bones! Get up! Get up!"

Binky slowly got to his feet. He patted his chest and his knees to make sure he wasn't missing anything. "Don't worry. I guess I was wrong. I'm as good as new."

The same, however, could not be said for the watch. Francine stared at the ground where Binky had fallen.

The crushed watch just lay there. It had been totally destroyed.

Chapter 10

• • • • • • • • • • • •

Francine turned to stare at Binky. A tear rippled down her cheek. She had suffered through the hardest week of her whole life. She had worked and toiled and sweated through one difficult moment after another. And here, at the end, her victory had been squashed along with the Princess Peach watch.

As the teams faced off again, Francine's face got redder and redder and redder.

"Uh-oh!" said Buster.

"Stand back," cautioned Arthur. "Give her room."

"There she blows!" said the Brain.

Francine didn't even hear them. In a blur of motion, she stole the puck from Molly and skated past Binky so fast he twisted his neck watching her.

She did a give-and-go with Arthur.

Score!

Then another one with the Brain.

Score again!

Francine passed to Muffy and Sue Ellen, and even got them passing to each other.

Again and again they fired at the goal. The goalie, Rattles, lunged to block them, but he never had a chance. He might have stopped Francine by herself, but Francine wasn't playing alone. She was the hub of her team, and the others were the spokes of the wheel. Together, they rolled over the opposition. Rattles got so tired of lunging at pucks that he finally fell down in a heap, exhausted.

Then the whistle blew, ending the game.

"We won!" shouted Francine as her team gathered for a victory cheer.

"We've got the old Francine back!" said Arthur.

"A new and improved Francine," said the Brain. "She actually let someone else score a goal."

Muffy shook Francine's hand. "Congratulations! I didn't think you could last a whole week. But I *am* glad you're back to normal. You were actually getting a little boring."

Francine gaped at her. "Me? Boring? What's the matter with you? If you think I'm boring—"

Muffy folded her arms. "Yessss?"

Francine suddenly relaxed and put her arm around Muffy's shoulder.

"I'll keep that in mind. Meanwhile, let's go find Binky. He owes me a watch."

Muffy paused. "How are you going to give him the news?"

Francine smiled broadly. "Very nicely, of course," she said, flexing her arms. "It's the only way I know."